ABBY AND TESS PET-SITTERS

Goldfish Don't Take Bubble Baths

★ BOOK 1

written by
TRINA WIEBE

illustrated by
MEREDITH JOHNSON

Lobster Press™

To my daughters, Olivia and Emily, and my son, Simon, who inspired this story by giving our own goldfish a bubble bath. – Trina Wiebe

Goldfish Don't Take Bubble Baths
Text © 2000 Trina Wiebe
Illustrations © 2009 Meredith Johnson

Published in 2009 by Lobster Press™
1620 Sherbrooke Street West, Suites C & D
Montréal, Québec H3H 1C9
Tel. (514) 904-1100 • Fax (514) 904-1101 • www.lobsterpress.com

Publisher: Alison Fripp
Editor, 1st Edition, 2000: Jane Pavanel
Editor, 2nd Edition, 2009: Meghan Nolan
Graphic Design & Production: Tammy Desnoyers

We acknowledge the financial support of the Government of Canada through the Book Publishing Industry Development Program (BPIDP) for our publishing activities.

We acknowledge the support of the Canada Council for the Arts for our publishing program.

The Canada Council | Le Conseil des Arts
for the Arts | du Canada

Library and Archives Canada Cataloguing in Publication

Wiebe, Trina, 1970-
    Goldfish don't take bubble baths / Trina Wiebe ; illustrator, Meredith Johnson.

(Abby and Tess, pet-sitters, 1499-9412 ; 1)
ISBN 978-1-897550-06-9

    1. Goldfish–Juvenile fiction. I. Johnson, Meredith. II. Title.
III. Series: Wiebe, Trina, 1970- . Abby and Tess, pet-sitters.

PS8595.I358G64 2009   jC813'.6   C2008-904635-8

Printed and bound in Canada.

Text is printed on Rolland Enviro 100 Book, 100% recycled post-consumer fibre.

TABLE OF CONTENTS

CHAPTER 1
No Pets Allowed

"The black one is the cutest," said Abby. Her nose was squished flat against the pet store window. "He must be the runt. Look how small he is."

"Woof," agreed Tess.

Every day Abby and her sister Tess walked past the pet store on their way home from school. And every day they stopped to look in the window. Sometimes they'd see a litter of kittens for sale. Sometimes there would be a new batch of hamsters or rabbits. Today, crammed between a dog food display and a stack of kitty litter boxes was a metal cage full of wriggling puppies.

"Poor little guy," Abby said. "The other puppies are stomping all over him. I wish we could take him home."

Tess tugged on Abby's arm and whined.

Abby stepped back from the window and gently pulled her arm free. She knew how Tess felt. They both loved animals. They had begged their parents forever to let them have a pet.

She shook her head sadly. "It's no use, Tess. We aren't allowed to have a puppy. You know the rules."

Tess bared her teeth and growled. Then she threw back her head and let out a mournful howl.

Abby sighed. Sometimes having a little sister who thought she was a dog could be embarrassing. She was always doing strange things like barking and drooling. Most people thought her doggy behavior was cute, but sometimes it got on Abby's nerves.

"Come on, Tess," she said. "We'd better get home before Mom starts to worry."

With one last wistful look at the puppies, they turned and headed down the sidewalk. They lived in the big brown apartment building at the end of the street, so they didn't have far to walk. Mom said that was one of the great things about being in the middle of town, they were

close to their school, close to the library and, of course, close to the pet store.

But Abby didn't like living there. In fact, she hated it. Their building was old, with about a million stairs to climb. The people below them played boring opera music in the evenings while Abby tried to concentrate on her homework. And the hallways always smelled like fried eggs and laundry soap.

Worst of all, there was that awful rule: No Pets Allowed.

As they climbed the stairs to their apartment Abby automatically reached around her neck for the string that held her key. They stopped in front of number 18 and she tried the doorknob. It was unlocked.

"Mom, we're home," called Abby as she opened the door with a push. She tucked the key back inside her shirt.

Abby's parents hadn't been sure she was old enough for her own key. It was a big responsibility. But now that Mom taught art classes at the community center she wasn't always home before the girls. This meant that Abby and Tess sometimes got stuck out in the hall. So after a lot of discussion, they decided to give it a try.

Abby knew she could take good care of the key. It was ordinary looking, small and copper-colored, like a million other keys, but Abby understood how important it was. She always kept it on a string around her neck, except at night when she slept. Then it hung in its special place on her bedpost, right where she would see it first thing every morning.

CHAPTER 2
Ordinary Abby

"I'm in the studio, girls," called Mom from the back of the apartment.

They dropped their schoolbags and ran down the narrow hall. At the end was a large bedroom that had been turned into a painting studio for Mom. You could almost always find her there. That's where she was now, seated on a stool in front of a large canvas, wearing an old T-shirt that used to belong to Dad.

"Hi girls. How was school today?" she asked with a smile as she looked up from the painting in front of her.

Abby shrugged and rummaged in the cookie jar until she found one with chocolate chips. The jar sat on a table crowded with paints and brushes and splotchy rags. "Okay, I guess," she said through a mouthful of crumbs.

"Woof, woof," barked Tess loudly, wanting attention. She climbed onto Mom's lap and nosed her affectionately.

Mom laughed and patted Tess on the head. "I see you're feeling quite canine today, my dear."

Tess cocked her head and looked puzzled. "Canine means dog," explained Abby. She knew a lot about animals. In her bedroom next to her desk was a whole shelf full of animal books. She had a lot to learn if she was going to be a veterinarian when she grew up.

Tess stuck out her tongue and panted happily. Mom laughed again and scratched her behind the ears.

"You shouldn't encourage her," grumbled Abby.

"She's just exercising her imagination," said Mom, raising one eyebrow at Abby. "There's nothing wrong with that."

"It's strange," insisted Abby. "None of the other kids in her class bark when the teacher calls on them."

"It's not strange," Mom said gently. "It's

different. Tess likes to express herself that way. Just like I express myself through my paintings. It's part of what makes us special."

"I think it's just plain weird," said Abby. Tess was on the floor now, scratching herself vigorously. "Besides, I think she has fleas."

"Well, we can fix that," said Mom. She scooped Tess up. "How about a flea bath? With extra bubbles, of course."

Tess yipped enthusiastically. Abby followed them out of the studio, shaking her head. She didn't care what Mom said. It just wasn't normal. Besides, if acting like a dog made Tess special and painting made Mom special, then what about her? What exactly made Abby special?

All evening Abby worried about being ordinary and dull. She thought about it during supper and later in the bath, a normal bath, not a flea bath. The more she thought about it, the more she began to suspect she didn't have any unique qualities at all. It was still bothering her when Mom came to tuck her into bed.

"Can I ask you a question?" Abby said in a

hesitant voice.

Mom sat on the edge of the bed. "Of course, Abby," she said. "What is it?"

"Well," Abby wasn't quite sure what words to use. She didn't want to sound insecure. Finally, she just blurted it out, "What makes me special? You have your painting, and Tess is imaginative, but what about me? I'm not special at all."

"Oh, honey, how can you think that?" Mom said, surprised. She smoothed back a lock of hair from Abby's forehead. "There are many wonderful things about you that are special."

"Like what?" Abby demanded. "I don't bark. I can't draw or paint like you. I'm just plain, boring me."

Mom pointed at Abby's bookshelf. "You're crazy about animals," she replied. "How many kids your age know the difference between a gerbil and a hamster? Or can identify twenty different species of dogs?"

"You think that's special?" Abby asked.

"Absolutely," Mom nodded. "You'll make a

great veterinarian one day."

Abby thought about it for a moment. Being a vet was the most exciting career she could imagine. "Thanks, Mom." She reached up and hugged her. Then she added hopefully, "I don't suppose that means you'll let me get a kitten? Just a small one ..."

Mom sighed. "Sorry, Abby. You know the rules here. Maybe someday you can have a pet, when we've saved enough money to buy a nice house with a yard. But not now."

Abby frowned and lay back on her pillow. As long as they lived in this smelly old building she'd never have a pet. How would she ever grow up to be a famous veterinarian if she never got the chance to take care of real animals?

Books were great for learning about animals, but they weren't the same as having one of your very own.

Chapter 3
Speedy and Slowpoke

Saturdays were the best. Abby loved to wake up knowing she had the whole day to do anything she wanted. Sometimes she got up early and went straight to the den to watch her favorite nature programs on TV. Sometimes she stayed in bed and read her animal books while Tess slept late. Whatever she decided to do, Saturday mornings were great.

But when Abby opened her eyes this Saturday morning, she found she wasn't the only one awake. Two big blue eyes were staring back at her, inches from her nose. They blinked. Abby rolled toward the wall and pulled the covers over her head.

"Go away, Tess," she mumbled. "It's too early to play."

Tess barked and pawed at the blanket.

Abby pulled the covers tighter and tried to ignore her. It wasn't easy, especially when Tess began snuffling near her ear. Finally Abby threw off her blankets and pushed past her.

"You're impossible," she said, irritated. Mostly it was fun sharing a room with Tess, but sometimes it was a pain. She tugged on her housecoat. So much for a nice start to her day. Maybe she'd go help Dad with breakfast. He usually made his famous blueberry pancakes on Saturday morning.

When she walked into the kitchen, Dad was stirring batter in a bowl and Mom was talking on the phone. Abby got the blueberries out of the freezer. She popped one into her mouth. Icy cold and delicious!

"Of course we don't mind," Mom was saying. "We'll be happy to do it. How long did you say you'll be gone?"

Abby filled a measuring cup with the berries and gave it to Dad. "Who's Mom talking to?" she asked.

He dumped them into the bowl and stirred

again. The berries made pretty purple swirls in the batter. "Mrs. Wilson from down the hall. She wants us to take care of her apartment while she's away on holiday."

Abby's mind whirled. Mrs. Wilson had an aquarium with two goldfish, Speedy and Slowpoke. This could be it, her big chance to finally take care of some real live animals. Well, goldfish weren't exactly her idea of fun pets, but they were close enough.

Mom hung up the phone and began setting plates on the table. Abby hurried to help with the silverware.

"Thanks, honey," Mom said with a pleased smile. "Where's your sister?"

"In the bedroom, being a dog," Abby explained. "She wanted to play, but I didn't feel like rubbing her belly again."

Mom chuckled. She handed Abby four glasses from the cabinet. "See? You don't need a pet. You've got Tess."

"It's not the same," Abby said. She put a glass next to each plate on the table. "How can

I ever be a good veterinarian if I never get the chance to take care of real animals?"

"Now, Abby," began Mom, "I thought we discussed this last night. The rule is ..."

Abby interrupted her. "I know, I know. No pets allowed. But Mrs. Wilson has goldfish."

"Fish are different," said Mom. "They don't make any noise or mess. Besides, you've never been interested in fish before. I thought you preferred mammals."

"Well, I do," Abby admitted. "But it would be good practice for me. So can I?"

Mom raised one eyebrow. "Can you what?"

"Take care of Mrs. Wilson's fish," exclaimed Abby. "I'll do a good job, honest. You won't have to remind me or anything. I'll feed them every morning before school. After school too. I'll clean their tank, and check their water, and ..."

"Slow down," said Mom. "I don't know about this. It's a big responsibility. Mrs. Wilson will be gone for a week. That's a long time."

"I can do it," insisted Abby. "I'm responsible

enough to have my own key, aren't I?"

Mom hesitated. "Well ..."

Dad laughed. "She's got a point there. Why not give her a chance? It's just down the hall."

Abby grinned. With Dad on her side she knew she could convince Mom. "Please," she wheedled. "I promise I'll be responsible. I'll do a great job."

Mom sighed. "Oh, all right," she said. "You can fish-sit. Happy now?"

Abby threw her arms around Mom's neck. "Thank you, thank you," she cried, hugging her tight. "You're the best mom in the whole world."

Dad put a steaming platter of pancakes on the table. "Okay, you guys. Enough talk. Abby, run and tell Tess breakfast is ready."

Abby hardly spoke during breakfast. She barely tasted the pancakes on her plate. She didn't even object when Tess lapped milk out of her drinking glass. She was too busy thinking about the job ahead of her.

The first thing she had to do was go to the library and take out books on goldfish. A good vet had to know all about her patients. Then maybe she'd stop by the pet store. They had tons of fish stuff there. She finished her food as quickly as she could.

She had work to do.

CHAPTER 4

Abby Loses Her Temper

Abby ran her finger along a row of books. She tilted her head sideways to read the titles. Finally, she spotted the one she was looking for.

"Find it, Abby?" asked the librarian, pausing on the way to her desk.

Abby pulled it off the shelf and added it to her pile. "Yes, thanks."

"Let me know if you need anything else," the librarian said with a wink. "You know where to find me."

Abby liked coming to the library. It was one of her favorite places. Of course, it was one of Tess's favorite places too. When Abby said she was going to the library for a while, Tess had insisted on tagging along. As usual.

"At least she's being quiet," Abby muttered to herself. She glanced over at the children's corner. Tess was curled up on a floor cushion with her nose in a book. For once she was acting like a kid instead of a dog.

Abby settled herself at an empty table with her pile of books. She hadn't realized she would find so much information on goldfish.

Her pencil made a soft scratching sound as she wrote in her notebook. She was surprised that goldfish could be so interesting. They liked cold water. They could live for twenty years or more. And even though they were called goldfish, they weren't always gold. Sometimes they were black or red or even spotted.

Abby was so involved with her research that she jumped when a hand touched her shoulder.

"Sorry, Abby. I don't want to interrupt you, but I think Tess needs some help." It was the librarian. She gestured toward the children's section.

Abby groaned. Tess was under a table, whimpering plaintively. Two small boys stood nearby, snickering. Abby pushed her notes aside. Trust Tess to find a way to disrupt her work.

By the time Abby reached her, Tess was growling. Abby shooed the boys away and crouched beside the table.

"Come out from there, Tess," she said in a calm voice. "You're being silly."

Tess ignored her.

Abby tried again. "It's okay, they're gone. It's safe to come out."

Still Tess refused to move.

Abby knew the librarian was watching them and she began to feel embarrassed.

"Knock it off, Tess," she whispered fiercely.

"Why do you have to act so strange all the time? Why can't you just be a normal sister for once in your life?"

Abby regretted her words as soon as they left her mouth. Tess looked stricken. Her face seemed to crumple and a small tear squeezed out the corner of one eye. Slowly, she crawled out from under the table.

"I want to go home," she said in a small voice.

Abby felt terrible. But now she was mad too. She hated it when Tess made her look stupid. "Fine," she snapped. "I just have to sign out my books."

Tess followed her to the counter, then out the door and down the street. After a bit Abby felt sorry and tried talking to her, but Tess wouldn't answer. She didn't say a word all the way home. She didn't even bark.

When they got to the apartment Tess went straight to the bathroom and locked the door. Abby didn't bother following her. Tess could be very stubborn when she wanted to, just like a dog with a bone.

Instead she went to her bedroom, dumped her books, then headed to the kitchen. Mom was sitting at the table with the newspaper and a cup of coffee.

"How was the library?" she asked, looking up from the article she was reading.

"Well," Abby hesitated, thinking of Tess in the bathroom. "I found lots of information about goldfish. They're not as boring as I thought."

"That's great, honey," said Mom. "Which reminds me, Mrs. Wilson left her key while you were out."

Abby forgot about Tess. "She did? Maybe I should go over there right now and check on Speedy and Slowpoke."

"Mrs. Wilson has only been gone an hour," said Mom, glancing at her watch. "I think the fish are okay for today."

"Oh, please," Abby begged. "I should really check on things. You know, make sure there's enough food and everything. Please?"

Mom gave in with a smile. "Suit yourself, Abby. The key is on the counter."

Abby grinned and grabbed the key. "Thanks, Mom. I'll be back in a flash."

CHAPTER 5

An Awesome Idea

When Abby was nearly at the front door, she had a thought. One of the books from the library explained about the different types of fish food. Maybe she should bring it along. It might be useful.

The books were in a heap on her bed. Just as she found the one she wanted, she heard a muffled sob. It came from the closet.

Abby sighed. The closet was one of Tess's favorite hiding places, especially when she was scared or upset. Abby went up to the door and tapped on it.

"I'm sorry, Tess," she said. "I shouldn't have talked to you like that at the library. I just lost my temper, that's all." There was no reply, but Abby could hear Tess sniffling.

"Look, I said I was sorry. Are you going to

be mad forever? Please come out of the closet."

Tess blew her nose with a loud SNORK. Abby groaned impatiently. This could take awhile. She looked down at the key and had an idea.

"I'm going over to check on Speedy and Slowpoke. Do you want to come?"

For a moment there was no response. Abby was ready to give up and leave. Let Tess pout in the closet all afternoon if she wanted.

But then the door slowly opened and Tess stepped out. Her eyes were red and puffy from crying. Abby felt bad all over again. She shouldn't have lost her temper at the library. After all, Tess was only a little kid.

She held out her hand. "Come on, let's go see the fish."

Usually Abby hated her little sister tagging along after her. It was one of her pet peeves. But if it made Tess feel better, this time would be worth it. Besides, they were just going down the hall. How much trouble could one little sister be?

Abby unlocked Mrs. Wilson's apartment

door and slipped the key onto the string around her neck. She heard the soft clink of metal on metal. Now two keys hung there. She wondered how many of the kids in her class were responsible enough for two keys.

Feeling very grown-up, she led Tess to the aquarium. It sat on a little table in the kitchen. Mrs. Wilson had let her feed the fish once before so Abby knew where all the supplies were kept.

"Don't touch anything," she instructed Tess. "Just watch what I do."

Tess panted, her puppy-dog eyes pleading with Abby.

"Nope. This is my job," said Abby firmly. "If anything goes wrong Mom will never trust me again. So hands off."

Tess growled unhappily but didn't argue. She turned to watch Speedy and Slowpoke swimming in lazy circles. Abby inspected the shelf under the aquarium. It was crammed full of boxes and bottles. She looked at the labels. Vinegar. Dish detergent. Baking soda. She knew the fish food was in there somewhere.

Finally she spotted a round jar with a picture of a fish on it. The label said Herbal Water Purifier. Nope. Abby pushed it aside. Behind it was another jar with a yellow plastic lid.

"Goldfish Flakes," she read triumphantly. She picked it up. The instructions were on the back. "Goldfish should be fed every day," she read out loud. "Feed no more than the fish will eat in a few minutes. Avoid overfeeding. Will not cloud water."

Tess whined. Abby could tell she wanted to be the one to feed the goldfish.

"Sorry, Tess," she said, shaking her head. "This is my big chance. If I do a good job with Speedy and Slowpoke, then maybe Mom will let me do it again sometime."

Abby stared at Tess, forgetting the fish food in her hand. What a great idea! Why hadn't she thought of it sooner? If she couldn't have her own pet, then maybe she could take care of other people's pets.

She could start her own business. She

could look after birds and turtles. Or hamsters and guinea pigs. Even cats and dogs. She would be around animals all the time!

She just had to prove she could do it.

CHAPTER 6

Bubbles!

Abby turned her attention back to the fish food. She pried the lid off the jar and pinched a bit between her fingers.

"Pee-yoo," she said, wrinkling her nose. "This stuff stinks."

Tess leaned over to catch a whiff. She screwed up her face and sneezed. "Woof," she said in disgust.

"Oh well, I guess they like it," said Abby. She sprinkled the flakes on top of the water and Abby and Tess watched as the goldfish swam eagerly to the surface. They gobbled up every speck.

"Do you think they miss Mrs. Wilson?" Abby wondered out loud. "It's so hard to tell. They sure don't look like it. But maybe they're really lonely and just can't show it."

Tess pressed her nose to the glass.

"Don't worry, Tess," said Abby, seeing the distressed look on Tess's face. "Fish probably don't even have feelings."

She watched Speedy and Slowpoke swim around and around in their tank. They didn't seem to notice much. They certainly didn't look sad.

"They don't care," Abby finally decided. "Fish aren't like real animals, you know."

Abby put the flakes away and went over to the sink. She found an empty jug and started filling it with water from the tap.

"I read that you should replace some of the water every few days," she said over her shoulder. "To get rid of the ammonia. If it builds up too much the fish will die. I'll leave this jug out overnight, and by tomorrow the water will be the exact same temperature as the water in the tank. Plus all the minerals and stuff will have a chance to settle to the bottom."

Tess was quiet, which didn't surprise Abby. There's not usually a whole lot of conversation when your sister acts like a dog. Abby hummed under her breath as she waited for the jug to fill up.

"There." She turned off the tap. "I'll just put this beside the tank. Tomorrow I can take some old water out and pour this new water in. I think I might even bring some lettuce. I read that goldfish like to nibble romaine lettuce. "Doesn't that sound funny?" she asked, turning away from the sink. The jug was heavy in her hands.

"But it's true," Abby continued. "You just hang the lettuce over the side of the tank ..."

Abby stopped talking. Tess was standing in front of the aquarium, blocking her view. She had a strange look on her face.

"What's wrong?" Abby asked nervously. "You look funny."

Tess whimpered.

Abby started to get a bad feeling. "Move, Tess. This jug is heavy."

Tess whimpered again. She stood with her back to the tank, her eyes wide. But she didn't move. Finally Abby pushed her aside. What

she saw made her mouth drop open. For a moment she just looked at the aquarium, speechless. She blinked.

"Bubbles?" she croaked.

There were bubbles everywhere. They foamed out the top of the tank. They ran down the sides of the glass. And they crept across the floor toward Abby's feet.

CHAPTER 7
Abby to the Rescue

"Tess," she cried. "What happened?"

Tess ran to hide behind a kitchen chair. She crouched down on the floor with her hands over her face. Her shoulders started to shake.

Abby glanced helplessly around the kitchen. She practically threw the water jug on the counter, not caring if half the water splashed out. She began yanking open drawers. She had to find some towels or washcloths. Even a sponge would do. Anything to soak up all those bubbles.

"Tess," Abby shouted furiously. "What did you do?"

Tess looked up. Her face was wet with tears. She began to hiccup. "I just wanted to make them feel better," she said in a tiny, scared voice.

"Who?" Abby demanded, not understanding.

"Speedy and Slowpoke," Tess hiccuped. "I just wanted to cheer them up."

Abby found the linen closet and scooped up an armload of towels. She flung them on the floor and frantically started to wipe up some of the bubbles. But the more she wiped, the more the bubbles spilled out of the tank.

"You said fish don't have feelings," said Tess, her voice wavering. "But I think you're wrong. So I wanted to make them feel better."

Abby couldn't believe this was happening. "Feel better?" she repeated.

Tess nodded. "I always feel better when I have a bubble bath. So I thought ..."

Abby felt her stomach clench. Goldfish probably didn't like soap in their water. What if they died? What would she tell Mrs. Wilson? How would she explain it to her parents? Her business would be ruined. She'd never pet-sit again. Ever.

Abby jumped up and stared at the tank. This was no time to lose her head. Bubbles foamed out the top in a steady stream. Thinking fast, Abby unplugged the pump. The aquarium grew silent. Bubbles still oozed down the glass, but slowly now.

She had to get the fish out of there. Speedy and Slowpoke were still swimming around, but she thought they looked a little weak. At least they were still alive.

She had to save them. She needed something to scoop them out of the water with. A coffee mug hung from a small hook above the counter. Stepping over the soggy towels, she grabbed it.

Abby took a deep breath and lowered her arm into the tank. The water instantly soaked through her shirt, plastering it to her arm. Frightened, the goldfish attempted to flee. They swam this way and that, avoiding the mug at every turn.

"Hold still," she cried. "I'm trying to save your lives!"

Abby dragged the mug back and forth through the water. Who would have thought goldfish could swim so fast? Just when she was

sure she had one cornered, it would flip its tail and dart away. Finally, frustrated nearly to tears, she captured them both and dumped them in the half-empty jug.

They were alive and safe, at least for now. Abby wiped some suds off her cheek and looked around the kitchen. What a mess. The entire room was a disaster. How could this have happened?

Her gaze came to rest on a green plastic bottle sitting beside the aquarium. She didn't need to read the label to know what it was. Dish detergent. And it wasn't hard to guess why it was sitting there. Tess was probably the only kid in the world who would think that goldfish liked bubble baths.

Abby looked angrily at her sister. "I can't believe you did this," she said. "I must have been crazy to let you tag along. Just look at what you've done." She gestured toward the aquarium. It was still foaming a little. "You've ruined everything."

"I'm sorry," Tess hiccuped.

"Never mind," Abby interrupted. "Just go home. I have to clean up this mess and get the fish back in their tank."

"I could help," Tess offered meekly. She crept out from behind the chair.

Abby glared at her. "I think you've done enough already," she said. "And if you tell Mom about this, I swear I'll never forgive you."

"But ..."

Abby lost her temper. "You always ruin everything for me," she shouted. "Would you just leave me alone for once?"

Tess left without saying a word.

Now it was just Abby and the goldfish. And the mess. She sighed. Somehow she had to get everything back to normal. If Mom found out, she could just forget about her pet-care business.

It looked like fish-sitting was going to be more work than she thought.

CHAPTER 8

Back to Normal

The first thing Abby had to do was get rid of the soapy water. She searched through the cupboards until she found a juice pitcher. Working quickly, she scooped the water out of the aquarium. Then she took out all the pebbles along the bottom and put them in a bowl to be rinsed. She did the same with the plastic plants and the funny little castle the fish liked to swim through.

Next the aquarium had to be rinsed out. Abby lifted the empty tank and carried it across the kitchen to the sink. She turned the tap on and washed away every last bit of soap. She scrubbed the glass clean, taking extra care in the corners.

She began filling the tank with water. It was almost half full when she realized she had a problem.

"I'll never be able to lift this," she cried. The aquarium was easy enough to carry when it was empty, but there was no way she'd be able to lug it back to the table full of water.

Exasperated, Abby scooped out most of the water. She carried the aquarium back to its table. Now it was ready to be filled.

"It's a good thing goldfish are cold-water fish," she muttered to herself.

This meant that all she had to do was get the water as close to room temperature as possible. A library book had said room temperature was 21 degrees Celsius. It was lucky the aquarium had a thermometer.

Abby lost count of how many trips she made to the sink and back. By adding hot, then cold, then more hot again, she was able to get the water to 20 degrees Celsius. Close enough.

Whenever she felt like quitting, she looked at Speedy and Slowpoke in the water jug. They didn't seem very comfortable. The jug was so small they kept bumping into one another. If they died she would feel terrible. For the first time

Abby realized that responsibility meant a lot more than just wearing a key around her neck.

When the tank was full she put everything back in. First the pebbles, then the plants, and last of all, the castle. Finally it was Speedy and Slowpoke's turn.

As gently as she could, Abby lowered the water jug into the tank. Slowly, slowly, she tipped it. The water from the jug mingled with the water in the tank.

"I sure hope this works," she whispered. "Please be okay, you guys."

Speedy and Slowpoke swam out of the jug and into the aquarium. Abby could hardly bear to watch. What if they floated belly up right in front of her eyes?

To her great relief, the fish seemed to be perfectly fine. They swam around a bit, exploring the corners and nosing the pebbles on the bottom. They looked exactly like they had before their bubble bath. Cleaner, maybe, but perfectly normal.

Abby looked around the kitchen and

groaned. She wasn't finished yet. With a tired sigh she began collecting the wet towels.

"Done," she finally said. Her hands were red and wrinkly. Her back ached. She'd never worked so hard in her life.

She stood near the fish tank and looked around. No one would ever guess what had happened. The floor gleamed brightly. In fact, it was probably cleaner than before. Abby hoped Mrs. Wilson wouldn't notice.

Abby could hear the towels tumbling around in the dryer. She would fold them and put them away tomorrow. Best of all, the fish tank was humming quietly, not a single bubble in sight.

"I'm sure glad you guys can't talk," Abby whispered to the fish with a tired grin. "Mrs. Wilson would probably faint if she knew what happened today. And I'd be out of a job for sure."

Speedy and Slowpoke just stared at her, their mouths opening and closing silently. Abby made sure their air hose was secure and shut the lid.

"I'll be back tomorrow," she said. "But don't worry, this time I won't bring Tess with me. I won't make that mistake again."

Abby locked Mrs. Wilson's door, then double-checked it just to make sure. She felt a little nervous.

What else could possibly go wrong?

CHAPTER 9

Divided in Two

As she walked down the hallway, Abby hoped her parents wouldn't ask why she'd been gone so long. But when she let herself into her apartment, she was in luck. It was silent.

She tiptoed down the hall. When she saw the Do Not Disturb sign on the studio door she breathed a little easier. Mom often lost track of time when she was painting.

"Tess?" Abby called. "Where are you?"

A muffled bark came from the kitchen. Abby found Tess at the table, eating a peanut butter and banana sandwich. One of her more disgusting habits, Abby thought.

"Where's Dad?" she asked, scowling.

Tess had to swallow a mouthful of sandwich before she could answer. "He went to the store," she said when she could speak again. "We're

out of milk."

Abby came right to the point. "Did you tell them what happened?"

Tess looked guilty. "No way. I swear."

"You'd better be telling me the truth," said Abby, "because the whole mess was your fault."

"Will Speedy and Slowpoke be okay?" Tess asked in a small, worried voice.

Abby glared at her. "Yes. I cleaned their tank and everything. But you almost killed them, you know."

Tess put down her sandwich. "I'm really sorry, Abby," she whimpered. "I didn't mean to hurt them. I just wanted to help ..."

"I don't need any more of your help," said Abby. "All you do is ruin things. You ruined my trip to the library. You nearly ruined my fish-sitting job. And I'm sick and tired of it."

"But ..." Tess began.

Abby interrupted her again. "I mean it, Tess. I'm tired of you always tagging along and bugging me. I'm tired of watching you act like a silly dog. And," she said, losing her temper entirely, "I'm tired of sharing a room with you!"

Tess said nothing. She just stared at Abby with wide eyes. She didn't even cry.

Furious, Abby spun around and left the kitchen. When she got to their bedroom she went straight to her desk drawer and pulled out a big roll of wide masking tape. She had used it last week to make a kite. The kite Tess had destroyed by using it as a chew toy.

Abby peeled the end of the tape loose. Starting as high up as she could reach, she made a tape line down the wall. When she reached the floor she pulled the tape across the carpet all the way to the door, pressing it down firmly to make sure it stuck. She stood up and looked at her handiwork.

The room was neatly divided in two. Her bed, bookshelf and desk were on one side of the tape. Tess's bed, toy box and dresser were on the other. Now Tess wouldn't be able to bother her.

Abby would finally be free of her strange, pesky little sister.

CHAPTER 10

Little Kids Are Strange

For three days, Abby didn't speak to Tess. Each time Tess tried to talk to her, Abby turned away or stared right through her. At night when Tess was in her bed on the other side of the room, Abby pretended her sister wasn't even there. Abby didn't want to walk to school with her either, but she had no choice. It was a strict family rule that the girls walk to and from school together every day. But that didn't mean Abby had to talk to Tess. Or even look at her.

Abby could tell it made Tess feel bad. Usually Tess was a noisy kid, always laughing or singing. Or barking. But lately she had been very quiet. She didn't tag along after Abby anymore. She didn't try and do the same things Abby was doing or bug Abby to play with her. Abby told herself she was glad. Things were much better this way.

Even the kids at school noticed something was different.

"What's wrong with Tess?" asked Abby's friend Rachel. They were standing near the basketball court at recess eating snacks from their lunches. "She looks like she lost her best friend."

"I'm mad at her," said Abby. "She's always bugging me and ruining things. I'm tired of it."

Rachel nodded. "I know what you mean. My little brother can be a pest too. Yesterday he took my favorite nail polish and used the whole bottle to paint his toy truck. I could have strangled him."

"She almost killed the goldfish I'm taking care of," Abby said. She crumpled her granola bar wrapper and tossed it into a garbage can. "She thought they'd like bubbles in their tank. Can you believe that?"

"Little kids are strange," Rachel agreed. "My brother thinks he's Superman. He won't go to sleep unless he's got his Superman pajamas on. Sometimes he even wears them under his clothes."

Abby nodded. "That's weird, all right. But at least he doesn't bark at strangers on the street."

"I think your sister is cute," said Rachel. She pulled her skipping rope out of her jacket pocket and started skipping backward pepper. The rope twirled faster and faster until it snagged on her heel. She stopped and caught her breath. "You should talk to her. You can't stay mad at her forever."

Abby frowned. She was still angry at Tess for almost ruining her plans to become a pet-sitter. Rachel was a good friend, but she didn't understand what it was like to live with a sister who acted like a dog.

As Abby walked home after school that day she thought about what Rachel had said. Tess trailed along behind her. They came to the pet store. As usual, they stopped to look in the window.

All the puppies had been sold. In their place was a hamster in a cage. At least Abby thought it was a hamster. Maybe it was a baby guinea pig. She couldn't really be sure because it was curled up in a ball, half buried under wood chips.

Abby opened her mouth to say something to Tess, then changed her mind. She wasn't ready to make up just yet.

Tess had to learn that she couldn't act so crazy all the time. Little kids don't bark. Or howl. Or scratch their fleas. And they certainly don't put dish detergent in aquariums.

The strap on Abby's backpack pinched her neck. She shrugged it off and slung it over one shoulder. They started down the sidewalk again. Abby's backpack was only really heavy on the days her class visited the school library. She thought about the books she'd found on fish. They were different from the ones she'd checked out of the town library. Maybe she'd learn something new.

When they reached their building, Mom was in the front lobby getting the mail. She had a magazine and a few envelopes in her hand. If she noticed the silence between Abby and Tess, she didn't mention it.

As soon as they were in the apartment, Tess dumped her backpack on the floor and disappeared down the long hall. Abby dropped hers beside it and followed Mom into the kitchen.

Abby grabbed an apple from the bowl on the table. "I'm going over to feed the fish."

"Are you taking Tess?" asked Mom.

Abby frowned. "Nope. She's staying here with you." She could tell Mom had noticed something was wrong.

It would be impossible not to notice. Abby had caught Mom watching them over the last few days with a worried look on her face. But so far she hadn't said anything. Abby was glad. She knew Mom wouldn't understand her feelings. She would be on Tess's side, as usual.

"Okay, just don't be too long. Dad will be home for supper early today," said Mom.

Abby headed for the door. She wasn't planning on being gone long. Fish-sitting Speedy and Slowpoke wasn't that much fun anymore. For one thing, fish weren't affectionate like other animals. Puppies wagged their tails and slobbered all over you. Kittens rubbed up against your legs and purred. But goldfish? All they did was eat and swim and stare at you through the glass. After awhile that got boring.

CHAPTER 11
So Very, Very Sorry

Every day for the last three days Abby had gone to Mrs. Wilson's apartment to take care of the fish. She fed them and checked their water and made sure they got plenty of oxygen. She even treated them to a few lettuce leaves. She knew she was doing a good job, but she wouldn't exactly call it exciting.

Sometimes it was even a little spooky. The apartment was so quiet and empty. Except for the refrigerator, which made strange knocking noises. And yesterday she could have sworn she heard a weird scratching sound coming from the bathroom. It was probably nothing. Still, she had almost wished Tess was there with her.

"Oh well," she thought as she walked down the hall. "Mrs. Wilson will be home soon. Then I can start thinking about my next job. Maybe a nice kitten ..."

When she got to Mrs. Wilson's door she reached for the string around her neck. Her hand touched bare skin. Surprised, Abby felt for the two keys.

They were gone.

Abby couldn't believe it. With a cry of dismay she grabbed her shirt and shook it,

hoping the keys would fall out the bottom. Nothing happened.

"I can't have lost them," she whispered frantically. She searched her pockets, though she knew she never put her keys in her pockets. She walked the length of the hallway, inspecting every inch of the carpet. They had to be here somewhere. They just had to.

What was she going to do? Today was Wednesday. Mrs. Wilson was coming home on Friday. The fish-sitting job was almost over. She only had to be responsible for two more days. How could this be happening to her now?

Abby couldn't blame this on Tess. Ever since that first day, Tess hadn't even asked to tag along. The only person Abby had to blame was herself. Suddenly she felt a little like Tess must have felt after squirting dish detergent into the aquarium. Helpless and upset. And so very, very sorry.

She hadn't meant to lose the keys. She didn't know how it could have happened. She was always so careful. But somehow, just like Tess, she'd caused a disaster.

"Okay, just calm down," she told herself firmly. She sat down on the carpet with her back against the wall. "I've got to think. When was the last time I used my keys?"

Abby closed her eyes and tried to focus. She'd fed the fish yesterday, so she definitely had the keys then. She remembered locking Mrs. Wilson's door. She also remembered putting the string around her neck this morning when she got dressed for school. So far so good. But after school Mom had met them in the lobby and walked up to the apartment with them, which meant Abby didn't have to use her key. Which meant she had lost her keys sometime between breakfast and now.

Maybe it had happened on the walk to school. Or in gym class while they were playing soccer in the schoolyard. Or while she was skipping at recess. Abby's heart sank. Her keys could be anywhere. How would she ever find them?

It was impossible. The keys were gone for good. Tears filled Abby's eyes. She pressed her hands against her face and forced herself to take a deep breath.

"It's not the end of the world," she tried to convince herself. "I'm smart. I can figure a way out of this mess. I just have to concentrate."

Maybe she could go home and pretend that she'd fed the fish as usual. Tomorrow she could leave the apartment and pretend to feed them again. Going without food for two days wouldn't kill them. Then she could say she'd put the keys back in the kitchen. Nobody would know she hadn't, and Mom might even think she lost them herself.

But that would be a lie. A whole bunch of lies. There had to be another way.

Maybe she could go to the building super-intendent and ask him to make copies of the keys. He had the originals, after all.

Except he would likely call her parents. And making new keys would probably cost a lot of money. Abby only had a few dollars in her pocket. She hadn't gotten paid for fish-sitting yet. And now she probably wouldn't get paid at all. She was out of ideas.

"I guess I'll just have to tell Mom that I messed up," she moaned to herself. She rested her forehead against her knees and tried not to cry. "This was my big chance to prove myself. And I blew it."

With heavy feet Abby went back down the hallway. She dreaded telling her parents what had happened. Even if they didn't get mad, they certainly wouldn't let her pet-sit again any time soon. Her wonderful plan was ruined. Destroyed. And it was her own fault.

Abby thought of the hard time she'd been giving Tess lately. Suddenly she felt bad. Sure, Tess had made a mistake. A huge one. But then again, so had Abby. Losing her keys had been an accident, but that didn't change the fact that she'd messed up too.

Abby decided it was time to have a talk with Tess. Especially before she broke the bad news to Mom. She would apologize for getting so angry and for staying angry for such a long time.

She just hoped Tess would forgive her.

CHAPTER 12

Getting the Scent

Abby found Tess sprawled out on her half of the bedroom floor, paging through a book. Usually Tess got Abby to help her sound out the words, but not lately. She glanced up when Abby walked in.

"I want to talk to you, Tess," Abby began.

"I didn't go over the line," Tess quickly assured her.

"That's not it," said Abby. She looked at the masking tape on the wall and carpet. "In fact, I think it's time to take the tape down."

"Really?" asked Tess. She looked puzzled. "But I thought you said ..."

Abby sighed. "I said a lot of things. Most of it wasn't even true. I know I hurt your feelings and I want to say I'm sorry."

Tess was surprised. "You do?"

"Yes," Abby nodded. "I shouldn't have said you're strange. That was mean. If you want to act like a dog, that's up to you. I shouldn't have tried to make you feel bad. I'm sorry."

"That's okay," said Tess.

"No it's not. I shouldn't have stayed mad at you for so long either. And as for this ..." Abby went over to the wall and began peeling off the tape. "Let's go back to sharing the room. The whole room."

"Are you sure?" asked Tess doubtfully. "What about the bubbles? I almost ruined everything."

Abby shrugged. "Everybody makes mistakes. Besides, it doesn't even matter anymore. My pet-sitting days are over."

"But why?" Tess cried. "It's a great idea."

Abby nodded sadly. "It was a great idea. A perfect idea. Too bad I went and ruined it all by myself."

"What do you mean?" asked Tess.

"I lost Mrs. Wilson's key," Abby admitted reluctantly. "Actually, I lost my house key too. Now I have to tell Mom and Dad. And I know what's going to happen. First they'll tell me how disappointed they are, and then they'll say I'm not responsible enough to pet-sit. I guess they'll be right."

"But you just said it's okay to make mistakes," Tess pointed out. "Maybe they'll give you another chance."

Abby crumpled the long string of masking tape into a sticky ball. "This was my chance. And I blew it."

Tess thought for a minute, then jumped to her feet. "I can help you find your keys," she said, panting eagerly.

Abby shook her head. "I haven't seen them since this morning. They could be anywhere."

"But you're forgetting something," Tess cried. She gave an excited bark and pointed to her nose. "My super sense of smell. Dogs can find anything with their noses."

Abby smiled faintly, but shook her head again. "Thanks, Tess, but I don't think that would help."

Tess put her hands on her hips and stared

Abby straight in the eye. "You said it was okay to act like a dog."

"It is," Abby protested. "I just don't think you'll be able to sniff out my keys. I'd better go tell Mom and Dad."

"Just give me a chance," pleaded Tess. She curled her hands under her chin like a dog begging for a treat. "If I don't find them, then you can tell."

Abby hesitated. Maybe it wouldn't hurt to look for the keys before she confessed her big mistake. Two pairs of eyes, or even noses, would be better than one. It was a long shot, but maybe with Tess helping her ...

"Well," she checked her watch, "we've got an hour before supper. Maybe we could look around a bit. I mean, sniff around."

"Woof!" barked Tess. She bounced across the floor and sniffed Abby's shirt enthusiastically.

"Hey, watch it," said Abby, taking a step back. "What are you doing?"

"Getting the scent," Tess explained. She sniffed some more. "Okay. Got it. Let's go."

Abby rolled her eyes but didn't say anything. Tess was a little off the wall, but Abby had learned her lesson. If Tess wanted to smell her shirt to get the scent, then Abby wasn't going to stop her. And if she actually found the keys, Abby would personally go and buy her the biggest, squeakiest chew toy she could find.

At the front door Tess got down on all fours and snuffled through the shoes and jackets. Their backpacks lay on the floor in a heap.

"Hey," Abby said, thinking out loud.

"Maybe my key string got tangled up with my backpack. It's possible."

Tess started pawing at the backpacks. They looked in them, under them and all around them. They checked the straps and zippers just in case the string had gotten caught. Tess even checked in her lunch box. No keys.

"Oh well." Abby's shoulders slumped. "I didn't really expect to find them anyway."

Tess wasn't discouraged. "Where do we go now?" she asked.

Abby tried to think logically. "I guess we should retrace my steps."

"Do we have to walk backwards?" asked Tess.

Abby laughed. "No, we don't have to walk backwards. We just have to go to all the places I've been to today."

"Woof," barked Tess. She bounded into the hall ahead of Abby.

CHAPTER 13

The Best Pet Ever

Together they checked every inch of the staircase. They found fourteen cents, three crumpled candy wrappers and a dirty blue sock. But no keys.

They checked every corner of the lobby. Eventually they made it outside their building. Abby walked slowly, scanning the sidewalk and the nearby grass. Tess followed behind, sometimes going down on all fours to investigate the ground under a bush or check a sewer grate along the curb. There was no sign of Abby's keys.

Finally they got to the schoolyard. Abby felt defeated. If they didn't find the keys here, they were almost certainly gone forever. Along with her chance to be a pet-sitter.

"Where did you play today?" asked Tess. She looked around the playground at the swings

and tetherball poles.

Abby glanced around too. The playground had never seemed so big before. "At recess Rachel and I were skipping over by the basketball court. And in gym class we played out on the football field. Oh Tess, this is impossible. We'll never find them."

"Don't worry." Tess squeezed her hand. "Everybody knows that dogs can smell a zillion times better than humans. I'll find your keys."

Abby tried to smile. She knew Tess couldn't smell any better than any other little kid, but she didn't want to hurt her feelings. "Okay. Why don't you try the football field. I'll check the basketball court."

Tess barked and loped off toward the grassy area behind the school. Abby's smile disappeared. If her keys were somewhere on that field, what were the chances of Tess spotting them? Probably a million to one. She knew she'd have better luck on the basketball court. At least it was smaller.

Even though she didn't expect to find

anything, Abby searched the area carefully. Twice she saw something shining in a crack in the cement and her heart gave a leap. But it was only the tinfoil from a stick of gum and the aluminum tab from a pop can. After awhile Abby knew it was time to give up.

"Tess," she shouted at the small figure running in circles on the football field. "Time to go."

"Did you find them?" panted Tess, breathless from running. Her tongue hung out one side of her mouth.

"Nope But we have to go now. Dad's coming home early for supper tonight."

"But the keys," objected Tess.

Abby shrugged her shoulders. "We tried, Tess. But they're lost for good."

"You can't give up," cried Tess. "Maybe someone turned them in to the office, or maybe if we look for ten more minutes we'll find them. We can't just quit."

"We have to," said Abby. "Come on, let's go. Mom's going to get worried."

For a moment it looked like Tess would

refuse. Then she scratched behind her left ear and fell in step beside Abby.

"I still think I could've found them if you'd given me a little longer," she grumbled. "I was almost sure I smelled them a couple of times."

Abby patted her sister on the shoulder. "Thanks anyway. At least we tried. Now it's time to go home and face the music."

"I don't think you'll feel much like listening to music," Tess said, giving her ear another scratch. "Mom and Dad will be mad."

"I know," said Abby. She didn't understand why she felt so disappointed. There hadn't been much chance of finding the keys. Maybe a small part of her had hoped for a miracle.

They walked along in silence, lost in their own thoughts. The only sound was a *scratch, scratch* noise from Tess. *Scratch, scratch. Scratch, scratch.* After a few blocks Abby couldn't stand it anymore.

"Would you please stop that," she cried abruptly. "You're driving me crazy!"

Tess quickly dropped her hand and stuck it

in her pocket. "Maybe I've got fleas for real," she said with a crooked smile.

Abby couldn't help it. She began to laugh. She laughed so hard she had to stop walking. She stood on the sidewalk, clutched her sides, and laughed until she could hardly breathe. Tess smiled at her, though Abby could tell by the look on her face that Tess didn't see what was so funny.

Slowly her laughter died down. When Abby was able to talk again she grabbed Tess by the arm and pulled her along the sidewalk.

"Come on," she said with a hiccup. "We're going to the pet shop. I'm going to buy you the best squeaky toy in the whole store."

"What are you talking about?" asked Tess, bewildered.

"Mom was right all along," Abby said. She swallowed a few leftover giggles. "I don't need a pet after all. I've got you, Tess. And you're better than any pet could be. Even if you do have fleas."

"Well, it might be a mosquito bite," Tess said.

"Whatever," Abby replied with a grin. "I

want to get you a present. To say thanks for helping me look for my keys. And for being such a unique little sister."

Tess still looked uncertain. But she followed Abby into the pet store. They headed straight to the squeaky toy display.

Chapter 14

Rubber Dog Bone

"Pick any one you want," said Abby.

"Really?" asked Tess.

"Go ahead," Abby said. "You deserve it."

Tess considered carefully. There were rubber hotdogs and hamburgers, big knotted sections of rope and funny-looking balls with soft spikes sticking out all over them. She hesitated, then picked up a large rubber bone.

"Can I have this one?"

Abby grinned. "It's perfect. We'll take it."

The man behind the counter took the bone and punched in the code. The name tag on his pocket said "Jeremy." "Did you girls just get a dog?" he asked kindly.

Abby dug into her pocket and pulled out all the money she had. "Nope. It's for my sister."

Tess barked happily. Jeremy looked

puzzled as he put the bone in a bag and took the money Abby handed him.

"You're a little short," he said when he'd counted it. "Do you want me to put the bone aside until you have the rest?"

Abby felt foolish. She hadn't expected this.

"Taxes," he explained.

"Will this be enough?" asked Tess. She stuck her hand in her pocket and fished out the fourteen cents they'd found on the stairs in their building.

He nodded and handed them the bag. "That'll do it. Why don't you girls check out the new bulletin board. You might find a puppy that needs a home."

"No thanks," said Abby with a grin. "Tess is the only dog allowed in our apartment."

They didn't even stop to look at the hamster on their way out. Tess clutched the bag to her chest and grinned from ear to ear.

Abby, on the other hand, wasn't looking forward to getting home. She knew she had to tell her parents about the keys. And she knew exactly what they were going to say.

Abby found Mom and Dad in the kitchen. "I've got something to tell you," she said, her heart pounding.

They looked at her expectantly. She cleared her throat. This was going to be harder than she'd thought. "I, um, lost my keys."

"You lost your keys?" repeated Mom. A frown creased her forehead. "Both of them?"

Abby nodded and stared glumly at the floor. "Did you look for them?" asked Dad. His usually smiling face was serious.

Abby nodded again. "We looked everywhere. I don't know where they could be."

Tess had disappeared under the kitchen table. Every now and then she made an odd thumping noise. Suddenly she chimed in, her voice floating up from under the checkered tablecloth. "We went backwards over Abby's whole day. I thought I almost smelled them, but then we ran out of time."

Dad looked confused. "Smelled them?"

Tess popped up and rested her nose on the edge of the table. "You know, with my super sense of smell."

"Oh, right," said Dad. "Of course."

Tess gave a satisfied snort and ducked back under the table. The thumping noises began again.

"We searched," said Abby, "but we couldn't find them. They're gone for good, I guess."

"Oh, Abby," said Mom. Abby could hear the disappointment in her voice. "We trusted you with those keys. How could you lose them?"

Abby had asked herself that same question a hundred times. "I'm sorry, Mom," she said with a helpless shrug. "I don't know how it happened. I guess the string broke."

Then Mom said the words Abby was dreading. "Maybe it was just too much responsibility for you. We thought you were old enough. Perhaps we were wrong."

"But I *am* responsible," Abby insisted. "I've taken care of Mrs. Wilson's fish every day since she left. I've done a good job. Losing my keys was just an accident."

"That's right," called Tess from under the table. "Everybody makes mistakes. Even Abby."

"I'm always very careful," Abby continued. "It wasn't my fault."

Tess popped up again. "Abby takes good care of Speedy and Slowpoke," she said earnestly. "She even saved their lives."

Abby groaned. That was the last thing she wanted her parents to know about.

CHAPTER 15

Everybody Makes Mistakes

"What do you mean, she saved their lives?" repeated Mom.

Abby shot Tess a warning look, but Tess kept talking.

"Speedy and Slowpoke almost died. But Abby was responsible. She saved their lives and cleaned up all the bubbles. You should let her keep her business."

"Bubbles?" said Mom.

"What business?" asked Dad.

"It's nothing," said Abby quickly.

"Abby's pet-sitting business," exclaimed Tess. She ignored Abby's panicked expression. "Abby wants to take care of people's pets when they go away and stuff. Cats and dogs and rabbits and ..."

"Okay Tess, we get the picture," Mom interrupted. She looked at Abby. "Let me get this straight. The goldfish you're taking care of nearly died. You lost the key to Mrs. Wilson's apartment. And you want to start your own pet-sitting business?"

It sounded bad when Mom said it like that. "Well, yes," said Abby. She looked at both her parents. She had to make them understand. "I know I made a few mistakes. But I fixed them too, at least most of them. That should count for something. How am I ever going to learn about responsibility unless I keep trying?"

Her parents were quiet for a moment. The only sounds in the kitchen were the strange bumps and thumps coming from under the table.

Then a violent thud shook the table hard enough to spill Dad's coffee.

"What on Earth are you doing under there, Tess?" demanded Mom.

Tess poked her head out between two chairs. Clenched between her teeth was the rubber dog bone Abby had bought her.

"What's that?" cried Mom, startled.

Tess spat out the bone and grinned. It bounced across the table and rolled to a stop in front of Dad. He picked it up between two fingers and examined it warily.

"It's my new chew toy," she said. "Abby got it for me. Isn't it great?"

"I hope it's clean," he said, handing it back to Tess.

"We bought it today," Abby reassured him.

Mom looked puzzled. "You bought this for Tess? Why?"

Abby shrugged. "I don't know. I just wanted to, that's all."

"I see," said Mom slowly. She seemed to be thinking about something. "I noticed the masking tape is gone from your bedroom."

Abby waited.

Mom glanced over at Dad and he nodded slightly. Abby felt her hopes rising. For some reason they didn't seem as angry as she had expected. She held her breath, waiting for them to speak.

"Losing those keys was a big mistake,"

Mom began in a serious voice. "It will cost money to replace them."

"I'll use the money I get from Mrs. Wilson," Abby said quickly.

Mom went on. "You'll have to explain to Mrs. Wilson about her key. That's part of taking responsibility for your actions."

Abby was ready to agree to anything. "I will," she promised.

"Having a pet-sitting business is a big job. People will depend on you. And it will be a lot of work. Animals are fun to play with, but they need to be taken care of properly."

Abby wasn't sure she was hearing right. "Does that mean I can do it?"

Mom hesitated, then glanced at Dad again. "I guess so," she said. "As long as you understand what you're getting into."

Abby couldn't believe it. Her parents were saying yes. They were going to let her pet-sit again. Even after such a disastrous first try.

She didn't want them to change their minds, but she had to ask. "Why are you giving me another chance?"

Dad explained. "Tess was right when she said everybody makes mistakes. That's how people learn. It's what you do to fix your mistakes that's important. I think you've shown us how responsible you really are."

"But how?" she asked, confused. "I thought I just proved how bad I am at responsibility."

Dad chuckled. "Quite the opposite, Abby. Think about it. You found solutions for your problems. You saved the goldfish. And when you couldn't find your keys, you came to your mom and me. That's what I call being truly responsible. We're proud of you."

Tess threw back her head and howled with delight. She began dancing around the kitchen. "Abby can pet-sit. Abby can pet-sit," she sang.

Abby's mind raced. This wasn't what she'd expected at all. She'd thought this would be the worst night of her life. Instead, she could start planning her new business.

First she would make posters and hang them up all over town. They would have her phone

number written on tags along the bottom that people could tear off and take home. Then maybe she'd make business cards ...

Suddenly she felt like singing too.

Abby started working on her first poster right after supper. Mom gave her some strong white paper and set her up at the easel in her studio.

First Abby penciled in the words. She used a big metal ruler to keep them straight. Then she colored them in with fat-tipped markers. Next she decorated the edges with drawings of different kinds of animals. She was just putting the finishing touches on a dog collar when Mom poked her head in the door.

"Time for bed, Abby."

Abby snapped the lid back on her marker. "Okay, Mom. I'm all done anyway. What do you think?"

Mom stepped closer to look at the poster. She read the words and smiled. "I think it's wonderful," she said. "Are you going to let Tess help you hang it?"

"Yup," said Abby. "I thought we'd stop at

the pet store on the way home from school tomorrow."

Mom gave her a quick hug. "She'll be so pleased."

Abby rolled up the poster, secured it with a thick rubber band and stuck it in her backpack without showing Tess. She wanted it to be a surprise. Then she got ready for bed. The opera music from the apartment below didn't bother her at all. She was sure she was going to dream about animals tonight.

CHAPTER 16
The Lucky Poster

The next morning Abby didn't say anything to Tess about the poster. They walked to school. At the end of the day they met on the front steps of the school and started home.

When they reached the pet store Abby stopped. "Let's go in," she said to Tess.

Tess looked up, surprised. "Why?" she asked.

"Oh, there's something I have to do," Abby said mysteriously.

"Are you buying me another chew toy?" asked Tess.

"Nope," Abby shook her head. "It's better than that."

Abby pushed open the glass door and they stepped inside. She wasn't interested in the new shipment of pet-care books, or even the hamster in the window. Instead, Abby stopped at the bulletin board.

She opened her backpack and pulled out the poster. She slid off the rubber band and unrolled it, bending it back a little to flatten it out. "Help me put this up, Tess."

Tess looked at it curiously. "You made a poster?"

"I'm advertising my pet-sitting business. I thought this would be the perfect place for my first poster."

"Woof," approved Tess. She stepped forward and squinted at the words. "What does it say?"

Abby grinned as she read the words out loud. "Going away? Need someone to look after your pet? Call Abby and Tess. We're responsible and reliable and our rates are reasonable."

Tess's eyes widened. "Hey! You said my name too."

"Sure," said Abby. "Having a pet-care business is a big job. I thought I might need a helper."

Tess stared at the poster. "You really want me to be your helper?"

"Of course," said Abby. "I know you love animals too. We'll make a great team. Now help me put this poster up."

The bulletin board was full of signs and notices. There was a photo of a lost Dalmatian with REWARD in big letters beneath it. Someone else was looking for a second-hand rabbit hutch. Tons of people had stuff for sale: dog houses and cat carriers and even chicken eggs by the dozen.

Abby and Tess found an empty space and put a thumbtack in each corner of the poster. They stepped back to admire it. The poster looked great.

"Let's go home and make some more," said Abby. "I want to hang one up at the library and one at the grocery store and maybe ..."

All of a sudden Tess went berserk. She started jumping up and down and barking like crazy. She pointed at the bottom of the bulletin board.

There, looped over a blue thumbtack, hung two keys on a frayed, dirty string.

"My keys," gasped Abby.

Jeremy noticed the commotion and walked

over. "Hi girls. Do those keys belong to you?"

"I lost them yesterday," said Abby, staring at the keys in amazement. "I didn't think I'd ever see them again."

"A customer found them on the sidewalk in front of the window yesterday afternoon," Jeremy said. He took the string off the thumbtack and handed it to Abby. "You must have dropped them on your way home from school. Say, is this your poster?"

Abby held the keys in her hands. Her mind

flashed back to the moment, outside the pet shop, when her backpack strap had pinched her neck. Perhaps the knot had slipped when she shifted the heavy bag to her shoulder. The keys were dirty, as if they'd been stepped on a few times, but they were hers, all right. She wouldn't have to replace them after all.

With trembling fingers she tied the string around her neck. She tied a double knot, then a triple knot. She didn't want to lose them ever again.

"Yup, that's our poster," Tess answered proudly. "We're starting our own pet-sitting business."

"Well, isn't this a lucky coincidence," Jeremy said. He scratched his chin. "My neighbor has a pet lizard. He needs someone to look after it for the weekend. Maybe I should give him your number."

Tess looked up at Abby, her eyes shining. "A lizard," she repeated in a breathless voice. "Did you hear that, Abby? We might get to look after a real live lizard."

Abby grinned at her. A lizard wasn't the same as a puppy. You couldn't brush its fur or take it for a walk. But it was definitely a step up from goldfish.

"Tell your neighbor to give us a call," Abby said. "We take care of all kinds of animals."

Tess chattered about lizards all the way home. "Could we go to the library and get out a book on them?" she asked.

"Sure, that's a good idea," Abby said.

"We have to find out how to take good care of it," Tess rattled on. "We need to know what it eats, what it drinks, how to keep its cage clean ..."

Then she frowned.

"What's wrong?" Abby asked.

"I was just wondering," Tess said in a timid voice. "Do you think lizards like bubble baths?"

Looking for more pet-sitting fun?

Be sure to check out all the books in the
"ABBY AND TESS PET-SITTERS" series.

Praise for the "Abby and Tess Pet-Sitters" series:

"... likely to tickle the funny bone of a young reader ...
reminiscent of Beverly Cleary's Beezus and Ramona."
— Quill & Quire

"A good read for pet lovers." — School Library Journal

"A really fun combination of weird animals and strong
female characters that deals with the themes of responsibility
and independence." — Kidscreen

"... a mix of animal information, sisterly dynamics,
and a lively plot ..." — Canadian Children's Book News